Gift f
the S

Gift from the Storm

AND OTHER STORIES OF CHILDREN
AROUND THE WORLD
Compiled by the Editors
of
Highlights for Children

BOYDS MILLS PRESS

Compilation copyright © 1993 by Boyds Mills Press, Inc.
Contents copyright by Highlights for Children, Inc.

Published by Boyds Mills Press, Inc.
A Highlights Company
815 Church Street
Honesdale, Pennsylvania 18431
Printed in the United States of America

Publisher Cataloging-in-Publication Data
Main entry under title :
    Gift from the storm : and other stories of children around the world /
compiled by the editors of Highlights for Children.—1st ed.
[96]p. : cm.
Stories originally published in *Highlights for Children*.
Summary: A collection of stories for young readers about children from
many countries.
ISBN 1-56397-268-9
1. Children's stories. I. Highlights for Children. II. Title.
    [F]   1993   CIP
The Library of Congress Catalog Card Number :93-70407

First edition, 1993
Book designed by Tim Gillner
The text of this book is set in 12-point Garamond.
Distributed by St. Martin's Press

10 9 8 7 6 5 4 3 2 1

CONTENTS

Gift from the Storm

By Kathy Millhoff

"Don't take those toys," I remember Mama saying. "We won't have room for them."

A sharp, sour pain hit my stomach as I carefully put away my dolls, dishes, and clothes. Would I ever see them again, or would they blow out to sea?

The night before, Papa had run into our small tin house by the beach and shouted, "The typhoon will be here tomorrow night! Condition Two!"

Condition Two was bad. It meant that our island

would be hit by the typhoon within twenty-four hours.

Right away, Mama had said, "We've got things to do, Lanita." She waggled fingers at me as she talked. "We've got to cook rice and breadfruit and then collect blankets, towels, candles, and matches."

We began piling up sacks of coconuts for Papa and my older brother, Diego, to load into our pickup. We wouldn't have drinking water for many days after the storm, but we would be able to drink the coconut juice.

Our island of Saipan in the western Pacific Ocean was often in the path of a typhoon. Preparing for storms was nothing new. Power and water supplies were usually knocked out during a storm, and wood or tin houses like ours were sometimes destroyed. That's the thing I would never get used to.

This time, something was different. I couldn't name it, but that sick-scary feeling was strong, and Mama rushed around faster than usual, her skirt flapping.

On the morning after Papa's announcement, Mama and I finished up the packing, while Papa and Diego hammered typhoon shutters over the windows of our house.

As the sky darkened, the wind began gusting harder and punching down banana trees. Far out over the ocean, thunder began rolling, sounding like a thousand giant coconuts bumping around.

Mama said again, "Lanita, there is no room for

those toys. Not even Maria."

Maria, my favorite doll, looked like an island princess with her wide, dark eyes and silky black curls. I'd loved her from the second I'd first seen her, when Papa brought her from Guam. I pictured her washed out to sea, and I wanted to cry.

"Condition One!" yelled our neighbor Vicente, as he drove past our house with his daughter, Taciana. She was grinning and waving. She was too young to remember how hot and stuffy a typhoon shelter could be.

Condition One meant the typhoon would be here within a few hours, so we took one last look around to make sure we had forgotten nothing. I took my chance while Mama's back was turned. I stuffed Maria inside a rolled blanket and put her in our pick-up truck. If the house blew down or flooded, she, at least, would be safe.

The shelter was our school, just up the road from our house. Mama found us a corner of the boarded-up library. We stacked our things along the wall and spread mats for sitting.

"You kids go get water," Mama ordered, handing Diego and me four one-gallon jugs. We joined lines of kids outside, all waiting to get water from spigots that were attached to water catchment tanks on the roof of the school. Most of the kids were fooling around, acting as though this was some kind of holiday. The lines moved slowly.

The wind blew harder, bending palm trees low, and the rain began in cold, stinging splashes.

"No more!" the call came back down the lines. "It's gone!"

Diego shook wet hair from his eyes and shrugged. "Come on, Nita," he said. "The tanks are empty." I stomped back to our cozy corner, angry because I'd gotten wet for nothing.

"Please help me," Mama said, frowning. She began pulling the outer husks from the coconuts. Now if we wanted a drink, we could just punch a hole in the eye of a husked coconut, and tip the sweet juice down our throats. Diego and I weren't fast at husking, but we began to help.

We were so busy we forgot about the storm. But when a howling, shrieking sound hit us like a million sea monsters tearing through the place, we were reminded.

The wind—we had to yell to be heard above its sound. It seemed to be everywhere, even inside me, although the library was closed and stuffy.

The energy from the storm made me feel all jumbled inside and as though I could fly if I jumped in the air.

Although we couldn't look out the shuttered windows, we heard the ripping, battering sounds the storm made. We could only guess what was being blown around. We were safe in the concrete school, but how safe were our houses, animals, trees?

The typhoon seemed to last a very long time. I couldn't sleep to make time go faster. That flying-away feeling wouldn't let me.

Hours later, when the wind began to calm down, the men went outside to inspect the damage. It was getting dark, and the moms wouldn't let us kids go.

Mama tried to get Diego and me to eat, but with the storm moving out to sea, I just wanted to sleep.

The next morning our island looked like pictures of it taken after World War II. Trees, wood planks, tin, glass, and power poles were tangled everywhere. It was as though a sea giant had picked us up, tossed us around, then gone off to play somewhere else.

The roads were so filled with debris from the storm that we had to leave the pickup at the school and walk to our house. That is, we walked to where our house had been. It was now just a pile of boards and tin.

Vicente's house looked like ours, and Taciana sat in the yard, crying, "My babies! My babies!" I knew she was crying about her dolls.

Being seven, Taciana could cry about such things. At ten, I knew that crying would bring back nothing. Not our houses, not even Taciana's doll collection.

We spent three more weeks living in the shelter, while the men and boys rebuilt the houses.

The Red Cross brought in food, clothes, medicine, and building supplies, and I began to feel that everything would be fine. After all, no one had gotten hurt, and we would be able to replace many of the things we had lost.

But when we finally moved the last of our things into our new, smaller house, I again saw Taciana sitting alone in her yard.

Taciana, who usually pestered us, jumping and singing and yelling, was now like an old sick cow, her head down and her hair covering her face.

"What's the matter, Ciana?" I yelled.

"My babies," she moaned. I remembered the day after the storm, when she had cried, "My babies!" She had not forgotten her dolls.

"Lanita! Lanita!" Mama called from the doorway. She was waving something and looking angry.

Maria!

I had completely forgotten my Maria in the busy days after the typhoon. Mama had said not to pack toys. I had disobeyed, and Mama was not happy. I walked to her slowly.

"Mama," I gulped, "I'm sorry I disobeyed you. But now Maria's a present for someone."

I took my doll, cradled and cuddled her one last time, then ran to Taciana.

I pushed Maria into Taciana's hands and said, "For you. Her name's Maria, and she needs you to take care of her."

I said it all in a rush, before I could change my mind, and Taciana's big smile was a kind of reward.

But when I turned back to Mama, I saw that for the first time in weeks she was smiling her sweetest smile. That was my biggest reward for losing Maria.

Anna's Summer

By Arnold A. Griese

My world of winter is a world of snow, and of cold, and of darkness. It is a beautiful time in Alaska, but for me it is a time of waiting. Waiting for the sun to warm the earth and to bring life once more to our frozen land.

At last warm days, pussy willows, melting snow, and ice breakup on the river all tell me that spring has come once more. The days pass swiftly now; the wild geese return, school is out, and then one day Mother and I make ready for our move.

Not long after, Father takes us in his boat to the place that is our summer home. Mother says that our people, the Athabascan Indians, have always come to this place in summer. Here fish swim close to the shore, berries grow on the hillside, and soft winds off the water keep the mosquitoes away.

Leaving the boat, I run up the hillside, then sit rest-ing. A fox runs past carrying food to his family. Far away, the mountain called "Denali" stands tall in the clear air. In front of me the river flows forever.

Mother's call stops my dreaming. I hurry back to the beach. From around a bend in the river comes the sound of hammering. Father is already at work getting the fish wheel into the water.

The open door, smoke rising from the stovepipe, and the rattle of pans inside the house tell me there is work to be done. "Anna," Mother calls again. I answer and go inside.

In the busy days that follow many things get done:

The cache is opened and its ladder put in place. Already food we brought from town is stored inside.

Heavy logs now hold the fish wheel out in the swift water. The water gurgles as it pushes against the paddles that turn the wheel. The wheel groans and creaks as it moves. I am glad it will be many days yet before the first swimming salmon are scooped up by the baskets and dropped into the fish box. Cleaning salmon is hard work. But Father needs fish to feed his sled dogs.

The empty drying racks stand waiting for the first salmon.

When everything is ready, it is time for Father to leave. His hand rumples my hair as we walk to the boat. He must go back to town to work. But he will visit us often.

Father leaves, and Mother goes back to work. I walk along the river by myself. A piece of driftwood is stuck on the beach at the water's edge. A push helps it on its way to the sea.

A raven calls from across the river. I sit to watch the clouds and to think. My eyes move slowly to the water. A beaver with a branch in its mouth swims past. It makes no sound. The quiet fills my ears.

On another day Mother walks with me. As we walk I watch, wonder, and then stop to ask, "Why is the world made like this?" She answers with a smile and with a brush of her hand on my hair.

Father comes to visit, to bring needed things, and to take back loads of dried fish that Mother and I have cleaned and put on the drying racks.

One day Mother sends me to the cache to bring the berry buckets. Now every day we walk to the hillside where the big blueberries wait to be picked. The sun warms our backs as we sit and pull the berries down into our buckets. Mother watches as some of the berries find their way into my mouth. The quiet is broken as she laughs. I laugh, too. Then it is quiet again.

Once while we are picking, Mother puts her hand on my shoulder. I look up, and her eyes tell me not to move. My eyes follow a sound. Something is moving. A bear eats berries and does not see us. Mother's hand stays on my shoulder as we crawl slowly back to where the trees hide us. Today the bear can have the berries.

One morning rain on the tin roof wakes me. Low, gray clouds fill the sky. The air is chilly. I snuggle back under the covers, but not to sleep.

Soon I slip out of bed, dress, and go out to walk in the rain. Ripe, red cranberries hang on the bushes along the bank. Their sweet smell fills the air.

In the days that follow, as we pick cranberries, other signs tell us summer will soon end. The days grow shorter, and the nights are chilly. The sky is deep blue, and the air smells different.

Mother starts packing. One last time I walk along the water's edge in the soft light of a full moon. The moon brings a special stillness as the warm light from Mother's lamp shines through the window of our house. I hear a loon call and think of what Mother has told me: that summer will come again as it always has ever since our people have lived by this river and fished on its banks.

Then one morning I hear the cry of geese. I leave my warm bed and stand outside the door. High in the sky long lines of wild geese call to each other as they fly to warmer places. I stand and watch and then run along the beach. The pebbles are cold under my bare feet, but I do not stop until a spruce hen flies up. Leaves on the birch tree in which it lands have turned yellow.

That same day the sound of a boat motor from across the river reaches my ear. Father is coming. Summer is over.

It does not take long to carry things to the boat and close up the house. The house stands alone under the trees as the boat swings away from the beach.

I take one last look. Then some of my sadness leaves as my head fills with things to come.

I sit bundled up in my warm coat and feel the wind against my face. It is good to be alive in this place.

The Reluctant Aeronaut

By Anita Borgo

Monsieur Bardet was the best wheelwright in all of Nantes. Maybe in all of France. It was Guerin's lucky day when Monsieur Bardet had chosen him as his apprentice. Even though he was only twelve, Guerin worked hard, and Monsieur said that he learned quickly. Soon he would make carriage wheels that were as good as the master's.

Yesterday Guerin had worked faster and more carefully than ever. Monsieur Bardet said he had done two days' work in one.

"Perhaps," Guerin asked in a whisper, "I may have a few hours tomorrow to watch the aeronaut?"

"The aeronaut? You want to watch a man hang from a balloon that is filled with smoke?" Monsieur scratched his chin.

"Yes, monsieur. I have heard of these magnificent balloons that rise into the air. Brave men hang from these balloons in baskets," said Guerin.

"No, you may not have a few hours," said Monsieur. "You may have the day." Monsieur tossed him a coin. "Make a proper holiday of it. Buy a sausage while you watch the brave man fly in his balloon."

"Nantes will be crowded," Guerin's mother had said. "And those balloons that look like floating moons must be dangerous."

Guerin reminded her that the aeronaut from England, Charles Green, had flown in a balloon for eighteen hours and traveled 597 kilometers without being harmed. And Napoleon, the emperor, had had five balloons floating above him when he was crowned. When Guerin showed her the coin that Monsieur had given him, Guerin's mother agreed that even a poor boy needs a day of fun.

Guerin's bare feet left prints on the dusty road. His mother had made him wear his new woolen trousers. Although his family was poor, Guerin had worn his best clothes to town. Nearby, two plow horses pulled a farmer's wagon. The farmer was also going to town to see the marvelous balloon, and he gave Guerin a ride.

Carriages, wagons, and people filled the streets as they neared the town. Guerin thanked the farmer and made his way through the crowd. He saw a poster that read:

July 16, 1843
Aeronaut Monsieur Kirsch
Will Fly His Montgolfier Balloon
Nantes, France

Guerin couldn't believe he was there. It was all so wonderful. Merchants sold cakes and sweet drinks. The spicy smell of sausages made Guerin hungry. He bought one with the coin. Guerin looked above the crowd and saw the giant balloon. It looked as large as the moon. It tugged angrily at the ropes that held it to the ground.

Guerin sneaked through the crowd to be near the marvelous balloon when it took off. As he walked, he smelled smoke and wondered what was burning. Then he remembered that a fire burned in the basket below the balloon to heat the air. The hot air then filled the balloon and caused it to float. Monsieur had explained it to him.

Guerin stared at the balloon. Suddenly it jerked. The crowd screamed and rushed away. Guerin couldn't see what was happening.

"It's free," someone shouted. "The balloon is free!"

Guerin turned and ran. Looking back, he saw the balloon coming closer. A giant shadow fell over him. It was the shadow of the balloon! Something clattered behind him. The anchor that had held the marvelous balloon dragged along the street. He felt a tug at his legs. The anchor snagged on Guerin's new woolen trousers. As Guerin ran, he pulled at the anchor to free it from his pants. The balloon jumped upward and pulled Guerin from his feet. Guerin fell and reached for the anchor's rope. He bumped along the ground, and then the balloon drifted upward. Soon Guerin floated a thousand feet above the earth, holding only a rope.

Guerin heard the cry of the crowd and, with his eyes tightly closed, felt himself being swept away. He forced himself to open his eyes. He saw people in wagons and on horseback rushing after him. The people were no bigger than ants. The town of Nantes looked the size of his finger. He felt thrilled and scared at the same time.

Guerin looked up. Two of the ropes that held the basket to the balloon had broken. The basket had flopped, and the fire was no longer burning. Guerin was hanging by the anchor rope that hung from the lopsided basket.

Flying freely, the balloon lost its anger. There was no longer a fire to warm the air that filled the balloon, which was coming closer to the earth. Guerin could see the Loire River. It looked like a silver thread running through the countryside. Guerin hoped he would land in the river. He was a good swimmer. If he landed on a house, he might get hurt.

As the balloon lowered, Guerin whirled around. He saw a haystack in a meadow. Two workers were eating their lunch on the haystack. "Help me, my friends! Come to my aid or I am lost!" Guerin shouted.

The workers heard the voice coming from the sky and saw Guerin hanging from the rope like a spider from a web.

"Never fear! We will save you!" one of the workers shouted. They ran under the balloon and held out their arms. As the balloon descended, a worker caught Guerin in his arms.

The workers took Guerin to his cousin's house nearby.

That night while his mother mended his trousers, Guerin dreamed of his adventure as a reluctant aeronaut.

• •

*This story is based on an incident that occurred on July 16, 1843, at Nantes, France, and which was recorded in the French magazine **L'Illustration** (Paris), Vol. 1 (1843).*

Mountain Mist

By Pam Sandlin

Tears welled up in Meg MacRae's eyes as she looked around her. Where were the trails and landmarks she knew so well? Only minutes before, her beloved mountain, High Crag, had been bathed in sunlight and Meg felt at home. Now the sun was blotted out by a low cloud. Almost immediately, the crag seemed dark and alien.

As the mist thickened and swirled around her, Meg wished very much that she had listened to

Mother. Mrs. MacRae had warned her not to come up on High Crag today.

"Hear me well, lassie," her mother had said. "The Crag will be smothered in fog and mist afore this day is through. Should ye climb there today, ye may not see to come back down."

Meg hadn't listened, and now her mother's words had come true. Worse than that, though, was an old Scottish tale that kept repeating itself in Meg's mind. Long ago her grandmother used to tell her stories of spirits and ghosts. One especially frightened the young girl.

When the mist has covered all,
And everything looks gray,
'Tis when the Kelpies come to call
And spirit you away.

Meg shivered as she remembered the verse.

"I'm not a wee lass anymore!" she said aloud to give herself courage. "Kelpies are only fairy tales!"

With a shake of her dark red braids, she started in what seemed to be the direction of home. Despite her show of bravery, her mind dwelled on kelpies as she walked. Kelpies were said to be evil water spirits that had the shape of ponies. They would graze on the banks of rivers and lochs. To see one was a bad omen. When someone drowned, it was said that a kelpie had carried him away.

Finally Meg reached level ground, but the mist was still there. It was so thick she could barely see the heather on which she walked. Not being able to see made every noise seem louder. Now that she was nearing the loch, she could hear each ripple of the water.

"I can't be far from home now," she thought.

A loud splash came from the loch. Meg jumped. Then she laughed at herself. A fish must have leaped from the water to catch a tasty bug. As another sound came to her ears, Meg grew pale. Clearly through the fog, there came the sound of hoofbeats. Meg panicked. Trying to stay by the edge of the loch, she ran desperately away from the sound.

"Meg MacRae, Meg MacRae!" The words echoed through the mist. The voice sounded strange and haunting to Meg's frightened ears. As she ran, she tried to remember if Kelpies had human voices. It seemed very unlikely. Meg slowed her pace to listen better. The voice rang out again, calling her name. It began to sound familiar. She stopped altogether and tried to call out, but her voice issued only a quiet squeak. Clearing her throat, she tried again.

"Who is calling for Meg MacRae?" she shouted into the mist.

"Where are ye, lass?" the voice boomed. "'Tis only I, Roy Dougal. Your mother's fair worried and sent me to look."

"Roy," Meg called in relief, "I'm here, by the loch."

"Stay put, lass," Roy called. "Keep speaking, and I'll find you in a twinkling."

The hoofbeats neared, and soon Roy appeared almost magically from the mist. He was astride his roan stallion.

Meg sobbed even as she tried to smile. "Oh, Roy!" she cried. "When I heard the horse, I thought you were a kelpie coming to get me."

"A kelpie now, is it?" Roy exclaimed. He smiled as he helped her onto the horse. "Don't tell me a lass such as you believes in fairy tales!"

"No, I don't. Not really," said Meg. "But everyone is afraid . . . sometimes."

One Cicada Summer

By Barbara Sherlock

You know when summer is coming, because the days get longer and hotter. In Australia, where I live, though, there's one other thing that tells me when summer has arrived. It's the noisy cicadas.

Everybody likes them. As insects go, cicadas are big, about three inches long. They don't bite or sting. They're not a pest to gardeners or farmers. Their bodies aren't delicate, like moths and butterflies, so you can handle them easily.

Most of their lives are spent underground, but when the first hot weather arrives, they climb up tree trunks on their long legs, shed their skins, and turn into handsome adult cicadas. Some are the color of the tree trunks. Some are the color of the leaves. The sound cicadas make is a queer mixture of drumming and rattling, with a sort of hiss as well. At first you hear just one or two cicadas calling, but before long there are thousands, all singing at once. Sometimes it's so noisy you can't hear yourself think!

Cicadas are important to me. As soon as I hear them, I know three exciting things will happen before long—my birthday, the long summer school holidays, and Christmas.

Some years there are more cicadas than others. The year I turned six was a really good cicada year, and I remember it well. The boys in my class were trying to see who could get the best collection of cicadas. (You collect them alive, because the best thing about cicadas is their noise.)

There are several different sorts of cicadas. Some, like the Green Grocer and Yellow Monday, are easy to find. Others, like the Cherry Nose and the Floury Baker, are harder to find. But the hardest of all to find is the handsomest. It's the Black Prince.

That summer, I'd found Green Grocers, Yellow Mondays, Cherry Noses, Floury Bakers—but not one Black Prince. Neither had anyone else in my class.

Then, the day before my birthday, Colin Evans came to school with a dead Black Prince that his cat had caught. A dead Black Prince is better than no Black Prince, so his collection became the best.

When Colin Evans ended up with a better collection than mine, I got cross and started wanting a Black Prince very badly.

All the kids in our street walked home together. There was me, Peter, Andy, my best friend, Michael, from next door, and Katy, Michael's big sister. Katy walked ahead of us boys and had to keep waiting for us to catch up, because we were all searching the trees for cicadas. Katy wasn't interested.

Suddenly we heard Katy call out, "Hey, everyone! Look what I've found!"

She was holding a Black Prince in her hand. Of course, we all wanted it, but Katy said, "You greedy lot. No. It's mine. I found it."

Michael said, "Maybe Katy will give it to me when she gets tired of it."

Why couldn't I have been the one who found the Black Prince? Thinking about it, I got crosser and crosser, until Mum sent me off to bed early. She said, "If your temper doesn't improve, I might have to cancel your party."

I'd been so busy thinking about Katy and the Black Prince that I'd forgotten tomorrow was my birthday.

As Mum kissed me and went to turn out the light,

I said, "Mum, I don't want Katy to come to my party."

Mum stood in the doorway and said, "Tim, there's something very strange about you tonight." She looked at me carefully. "Yes, I know what it is. You've changed color. You're green!" I looked down at my arms. They didn't look green to me.

Mum came and sat on my bed. "There's a saying people use," she said. "They say someone is green with jealousy. That's what you are just now. You're jealous that Katy's got the Black Prince. Just now, Tim, you're not acting very nicely."

I didn't say anything, but I sure didn't like it when Mum said I wasn't very nice.

"One more thing," said Mum. "Did Katy really do anything to you?"

I sighed. "No, Mum, I guess she didn't. She found that cicada, and it's really hers."

"There you are," said Mum. "I hope you'll be your own color in the morning."

In the morning I wasn't green. Katy was lucky to have the Black Prince, but maybe if I kept looking, I'd find one, too.

I forgot about cicadas in the excitement of my birthday. I got presents from my family in the morning, and in the afternoon my friends came to the party. Michael and Katy were the last to arrive. I unwrapped Michael's present. It was a water pistol. Then Katy gave me hers.

It was a shoe box. It wasn't wrapped in birthday paper, but there was a bright yellow ribbon around it. It felt so light that I wondered if Katy was playing a trick on me.

I pulled the ribbon, lifted off the lid—and there was the Black Prince. Joyfully, I looked at Katy.

"Happy birthday, Tim," she said. "I thought something with six legs was a good present for someone six years old."

That summer there were lots more cicadas captured, but only one other boy in my class found a Black Prince. And since he didn't have a Cherry Nose, my collection—thanks to Katy—was the best one of all.

The Lighted Beach

By Aure Sheldon

Lightning cracked sharply, followed by a violent roll of thunder that echoed from the rocky cliffs above the shore. A heavy gray cloud shadowed land and sea. Always, Marcel would wait until he saw his father's boat coming in before he went home, but today he must not. He knew the sudden fury of late summer thunderstorms along the Gaspé shore on the Canadian coast.

From the highway above, he could see the little

weathered cottages of his friends and neighbors, the codfish curing on long racks near the beach, and the big nets spread out to be mended. All of the fishing boats except his father's were already docked. He scanned the angry sea, hoping to see the *Mouette* bobbing in the large swells.

"I wonder what is keeping them." He spoke to the big, old Labrador dog, Napoleon, his only companion during the long days he spent above the village selling his hand-carved wooden sailboats to tourists. He longed to be grown-up enough to work with his father and older brothers on the fishing boat! The dog licked Marcel's hand and whined softly. Swept from the windy sky, the last gull flew inland, screaming a protest.

"I hope they get in soon," said Marcel. To his relief, the beam from the lighthouse across the little harbor began to flash in steady rhythm.

"Hold still, Napoleon," he said, hitching the dog quickly to the wooden cart. Carefully, he loaded the unsold boats. "Eighteen left. We did not do well today, *mon ami.*"

As Marcel fastened an old piece of sailcloth over the top of the cart, the first slanting drops of rain struck his face. He put on his beret and headed toward home, beckoning Napoleon to follow. A bolt of lightning rent the air with a blinding flash. Both boy and dog trembled. Marcel clutched at the dog's harness and patted his head to quiet him. When he looked again toward the lighthouse, he was struck with horror.

"The light! The light is out!" Marcel yelled. There were no lights anywhere in town. "That lightning must have struck the transformer. Come, Napoleon, we must run!"

Marcel raced for the village. His fears mounted with every step. The wind slackened now, but rain came as if poured from a pitcher. Marcel could see only a few feet ahead.

"Faster, *mon vieux,* faster!" he urged. His bare feet now scarcely touched the ground as he raced down the long slope of the highway. The booming thunder all but smothered the sound of his voice as he called out to each house he passed, "Turn out, turn out! The light is out. Bring firewood!"

People hurried from the houses. Their oilskins flapped in the wind as they tried to buckle them up on the run. Marcel did not stop but raced straight to the beach, Napoleon close at his heels.

Daniél was the first boy to reach his side. Marcel had to shout at him to be heard above the noise of the storm. "We must build fires along the shore. The *Mouette* is not in yet!"

"Fires?" cried Daniél. "How can we start a fire without even one stick of dry kindling?"

Marcel fumbled with the clasp that held the cover over the cart. Loosening one corner, he reached under and pulled out several of the boats that he and his father had made with so much pride and care during the winter.

"Here," he said, piling them on the beach and leaning over to shield them from the pounding rain. "These will get a strong flame started, then our firewood will keep it going."

"But your boats, Marcel," protested Daniél.

"We can make more boats," answered Marcel firmly as he touched a match to them. "It is only my father's boat that matters now." The flame flickered, then caught, and the boats burned brightly despite the rain. "Quickly, put some wood over them and then follow me, Daniél."

Marcel ran down the beach, reached into the cart for more of the precious boats, and kindled another fire. As soon as he had each fire started, the towns-people fed it firewood from their own woodpiles. Not until Marcel had used up the last of the boats did he stop to look back. Five fires glowed along the shore like bright beacons in the deepening gloom.

The people who had gathered on the beach huddled together in small groups. They looked anxiously toward the sea. They all hoped to catch sight of the *Mouette*. Everyone had the same thought —the jagged reefs along the coast had caused so many shipwrecks in years gone by.

Suddenly, a man called out, "I see her. Over there, not far from the reefs."

A flash of lightning outlined the boat for an instant, and Marcel saw her rising high on the crest of one huge wave, then disappearing into the trough of another.

"More wood! Bring dry wood and feed the fires! Light your lanterns!" shouted Marcel.

What had been little more than a shadow of a boat became more distinct as the *Mouette* drew closer. Finally, she could be seen coming around the outer reefs right on course. Marcel noticed that she was riding very heavily, and he wondered if she was taking on water. Still, she was almost in the harbor now, and his fears for her safety gave way to a new anxiety. He turned toward his mother, who was standing nearby, tense and silent.

"Will Papa be angry because I burned the boats?" Marcel ventured.

"No. I'm sure that he will be proud of you," she replied.

And so it was. Later, when the *Mouette* was safely docked, rain-soaked friends gathered around the kitchen at Marcel's house for chowder and slices of brick-oven bread. Then his father and older brothers heard the story of how Marcel had started the fires. Father put his hand on Marcel's shoulder.

"Marcel, my son," he said, "had it not been for your fires along the shore, we'd have lost the biggest catch we've ever made. Without the big light to give us a bearing, we did not realize that we were as close to the shore as we were. We were just about to cut loose the nets so that we could move faster when we saw the fires. You have shown us all that you are too brave and grown-up to sell toy boats. How would you like to work on the *Mouette* with your brothers and me?"

"I would like that very much," said Marcel. He glowed inside as brightly as five beach fires had glowed on a stormy coast.

The Sirocco

By Fletcher J. Eller and Pearl K. Eller

Leyla was scared. A hot, dry wind was blowing across the Sahara Desert. Uncle Mustafa had told her that siroccos could happen in this kind of weather.

The thought made her shiver despite the heat. Leyla looked at the horizon. Sure enough, fine sand was darkening the sky.

Leyla had learned in fourth grade about the dangerous windstorms called siroccos, but she never dreamed she might actually get caught in one.

Why, she wondered, had she ever talked her

parents into letting her spend the summer on her uncle's farm? She should have stayed in the city. There were no siroccos in Casablanca.

And why hadn't she stayed on the farm today to help Aunt Suella make goat-milk cheese? Instead, she had insisted on going to the oasis with Cousin Beloch to pick dates. She was sorry she had been so stubborn.

"Hurry up, Leyla," Beloch told her. "We're going to get caught in the sirocco. Father will be worried."

The sand was beginning to swirl at their feet. Even Beloch, who was three years older and had been raised in the desert, looked scared. "Why did you have to come along, anyway?" he asked crossly. "I don't need a cry-baby girl to look after."

"You don't have to look after me. I'm big enough to take care of myself," answered Leyla. Her dark brown eyes flashed. "Help me back on Selma."

Selma, the camel, carried the baskets of sweet, juicy dates. They had stopped for a snack of dates and warm camel's milk on their way back home. Now they must hurry.

"Put your foot in my hands so I can boost you up," said Beloch.

But before Leyla could remount, Selma bolted like a streak of lightning. Both Beloch and Leyla were knocked to the ground by the runaway camel.

Beloch hit the ground with a thud. Leyla saw that his head had struck a rock that jutted from the ground.

Beloch lay still. The camel was gone, and the desert was now silent except for the roar of the wind.

"Beloch! Beloch! Get up. Please get up!" yelled Leyla.

Kneeling down beside his tall, suntanned body, shaking him and patting his face, Leyla cried, "Wake up, Beloch! I'm scared!" Tears ran down her dusty cheeks, now burning from the stinging, blowing sand. The sand was so thick that she could barely see.

Beloch was still unconscious. Leyla took off her long, hooded cloak and threw her body over Beloch face. She pulled the cloak over both of them to protect them from the flying sand that had felt like pellets bouncing off her face.

The wind shrieked and blew sand over them. Leyla closed her eyes and held Beloch tightly.

"Please let Beloch be all right," she thought to herself. "And please don't let the sand bury us alive."

Leyla lay still for what seemed like hours. Her whole body felt numb. Finally, the wind stopped. Leyla cautiously lifted the cloak and found that she could see again. She and Beloch were completely covered with sand.

But they were not buried. She was able to jump up and knock the sand off herself. Frantically, she began brushing it off Beloch. He moaned and began to stir.

"Come on. Get up! The storm is over!" Leyla yelled.

Beloch sat up slowly and brushed the sand from his black hair. He rubbed the back of his head and made a face. Looking around, he saw the sun in a clear blue sky. There was no wind, and no blizzard of sand.

"Little cousin, you saved my life. If you hadn't covered me up, I would have suffocated from the sand," said Beloch. "You are a brave girl, and I'm grateful to you."

"I'm just happy it's over," said Leyla, smiling. She combed the sand from her hair.

"We had better hurry home," said Beloch. "The sun will go down soon."

Beloch took Leyla by the hand, and together the cousins started walking toward home.

"What a scare it was," thought Leyla. "Wait until I tell the kids at school about being caught in a sirocco!"

It was dark when they arrived home. Uncle Mustafa was about to go searching for them.

"How happy I am to see you!" he cried. "Selma came home by herself, and I thought something terrible had happened to you. Come in and have some supper."

After a warm, soapy bath and several helpings of delicious lamb couscous, Leyla smiled as Beloch told his parents for the third time about how brave she had been.

The sirocco had also visited the farm. It had damaged part of the barn roof, and many tree limbs had blown into the yard.

Tomorrow the cleanup would begin, but tonight Leyla felt only happiness. She was content to sip a tall glass of fresh mint tea, and to thank Allah for the safety of all of them.

Thursday Is Market Day

By Jean McLeod

Ten-year-old Elena ran out of the brown mud house. She shivered in the early morning air and hurried to the side of the house. There Rosita, the family llama, neck bent over to the ground, chewed contentedly on a small clump of grass. She raised her head as Elena approached.

"It's Thursday, Rosita," said Elena. "You have to go to market with us. You will carry the blankets and potatoes. Come on." Elena put her arm around Rosita's long, fluffy neck and led the gentle animal around to the front door.

Behind the house she could see the glow of the rising sun. Here in the high Andes Mountains of Peru in South America, Elena lived with her parents and brother, fourteen thousand feet above sea level.

Many houses made of baked mud and grass, called adobe houses, dotted the mountainside. The people grew potatoes in small fields and herded llamas around their homes, much as their ancestors had done for centuries before them.

Every Thursday the people in the high areas would travel down to the town of Chupaca (chew PAH kah) to sell potatoes and hand-woven blankets made from the wool of the llamas. They used the money they received to buy beans and tea, sewing needles and pots, things they could not grow or make.

Elena loved Thursdays. While her brother and father stayed behind to watch over the llamas and work the land, Elena and her mother would walk for two hours down to market to sell what they had and to buy what they needed. It was also a time to see friends.

Elena's mother now stood at the front door holding two wool saddlebags stuffed with small potatoes. She flung the potato bags onto the llama's back while Elena held Rosita still. Next, she strapped on four blankets. Rosita twisted her long, elegant neck around to see the load.

"Rosita, don't complain," said Elena. "Mama didn't give you a heavy load. You can easily carry that much."

Elena's mother laughed, petting the llama's head. "Get along now. Show us your strong, proud walk." Rosita turned and strutted across the yard toward the path that would lead down the mountain to the town below.

Elena's mother placed two more blankets in her manta (MAHN tah), a large square of colorful cloth used to carry loads on her back. Elena filled her own manta with extra potatoes that did not fit into the saddlebags on Rosita's back. The mother and daughter quickly moved to catch up with the llama, and the trio started their long trek down to Chupaca on the well-trodden path.

The sun was higher in the sky now, and Elena felt warm and happy. The closer they came to the town, the more they joined other people and llamas going to market. Finally, as Elena and her mother crossed over a ridge, they spotted the miniature town below. It would still take time to wind their way down to Chupaca and the busy market.

The marketplace, located in a large field, already overflowed with people as Elena and her mother arrived.

"*Hola*, Lucia. I will come see you later," said Elena as she walked by one booth.

Elena's mother found an empty space on the ground. She unloaded Rosita. Then Elena led her llama to the public corral.

Elena skipped back to the place where her mother sat chatting with another woman in Quechua (KETCH wuh), the language of her people. With beautiful blankets displayed beside her and the potatoes spread out in front of her, Elena's mother settled into the market scene.

Elena took off her manta and placed her own load of potatoes next to her mother's pile. She sat down to rest and to watch the people pass by. The large field swarmed with activity.

"Hey, *chica,* how much are you asking?" An old man stood in front of her, reaching down to touch the potatoes.

Elena looked up. "You can have them for eight *soles* (SOUL lace). That is a good price," she said.

The man frowned. "But your potatoes are small. I don't think they are worth that. I'll give you four *soles,*" he said.

Elena glanced over to her side, but her mother could not help. She, too, had a customer and was try-ing to settle on the price of a blanket. There were no fixed prices in the marketplace. Seller and buyer tossed out prices to each other until they could agree on a price or the customer walked away. Elena did not want this customer to leave.

She looked at the man, "These potatoes may be small, but they are fresh. We dug them up only yesterday. I would sell them to you for seven *soles.*"

The man shrugged his shoulders. "That is still too high," he said. "I'll give you six *soles*. My last offer."

"OK," said Elena, "you are getting some good potatoes cheap. Let me put them in your bag." The man counted out six coins and opened up his cloth bag for Elena to fill. He walked away.

Elena smiled. Her mother was still haggling with a woman over the price of a blanket, so she walked over to find her friend Lucia. The two girls strolled through the marketplace.

When the sun started to lower in the sky, Elena returned to her mother's side. "Mama, I sold my potatoes for six *soles*," Elena exclaimed as she held out the coins.

"That's good, Elena. You have learned to bargain well. I am proud of you," her mother said, smiling at her daughter. "I, too, sold my potatoes and two blankets. We must soon be on our way. While I buy some supplies, please get Rosita from the corral."

There were fewer llamas in the corral as Elena approached. The mountain people were starting to pack up and leave. Soon the sun would go down behind the hills to the west. By then, Elena and her mother, with Rosita, would be on the narrow, winding path, hiking back up to their own adobe home.

The Storyteller

By Lissa Reidel

In Marrakech they call it the Djemaa el Fna, which means the Square of the Dead, but the huge plaza is bursting with life. From all over Africa come snake charmers and fortune-tellers, dancers and musicians, merchants loaded with silver and gold, and Berber women selling fresh, hot bread. And that's during the day. In the evening the square really lights up! Suddenly outdoor restaurants seem to appear from nowhere—tables and benches and steaming pots of couscous, chicken, potatoes, lamb, and beans.

At one of these tables Hamid is serving soup. Every night Hamid helps his father in their restaurant. It is near the place where the storytellers and the magicians entertain the crowd. Hamid's family is known for its soup and has regular customers. Hamid works hard cooking and serving. He's good at his work, and his father has made him a promise. When Hamid grows up, the restaurant will be his.

Hamid the Soup Server has other hopes, other dreams. He has lived by this square for as long as he remembers. He has carried pots of soup every night since he was old enough to carry anything. He has served bowls of soup to friends and strangers, smiling and talking.

"Enough is enough," Hamid told his father one day. "I don't want to serve soup all my life."

His father filled another bowl and handed it to him. "What will you do?" he asked. "Will you run in the streets, getting into trouble? You have no other trade."

"I will be a storyteller," Hamid said. Now in Marrakech good storytellers are popular. If people want to hear the history of the old days, stories of love and courage, tales of adventure, they gather in a circle at the feet of a storyteller. And he not only tells the story but also acts out each part with talent and humor. In Marrakech such entertainment is considered better than television.

"A storyteller!" lamented Hamid's father. "What do you know of such things?"

"I don't know anything yet, but I want to learn," said Hamid. "Mokhtar the Great has agreed to let me help him in his storytelling, and in that way I will learn the art of a great man. But I must have your permission to go."

Hamid's father was reluctant. He needed Hamid's help to run his business. But he loved Hamid and wanted him to be happy. He thought it over and made a decision. "Your brother can help me for the next two months," he told Hamid. "You have that much time to learn your new trade and convince me that you have the talent to make a living as a storyteller."

Hamid hugged his father and then hurried off in search of Mokhtar.

Hamid not only worked with Mokhtar, he also lived with him. Now and then Hamid's family would catch a glimpse of him with the storyteller, acting a part or holding out a hat while the crowd tossed coins.

After two months Hamid returned to the restaurant. He tied on his apron and started dishing out soup. The old customers welcomed him back.

"So, Son, it didn't work out," his father said kindly. "Well, you always have work here in the family business."

Suddenly Hamid threw off his apron and reached

under the table. He pulled out a bag from which he took a hat and a long stick. With a flourish he lowered his voice and said, "Come one, come all! Hear the famous story told during an Arabian night long ago, a story of cowardly spies and one brave young lady and the prince she loved and the kingdom she saved."

Hamid's father put down his ladle. The customers put down their soup spoons. People passing by slowed down and stopped.

While Hamid told his story, no one moved. The soup simmered in the pots and cooled in the bowls. People forgot they were in the Djemaa el Fna. They went with Hamid to an Arabian night long ago when a brave maiden saved the kingdom.

When Hamid was finished, the crowd applauded, and Hamid passed his hat. It filled with coins.

Hamid's father was astonished. He was the first to admit it. Hamid the Soup Server had become Hamid the Storyteller.

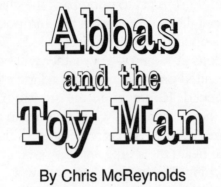

Abbas
and the
Toy Man

By Chris McReynolds

Abbas walked slowly down the dirt road from school, his bare feet squishing in the hot dust. There were no paved streets in his Iranian village. He carried his shoes, for he wanted them to last a long time. Shoes cost many *tomans*.

Water flowed in the ditch beside the road. Abbas stopped to cool his feet in the gurgling stream.

Abbas's mother waited at the compound gate. She

had forgotten to buy *sangak*, the bread his father liked. And it was lunchtime.

"Run to the bake shop and get three sheets of *sangak*," she said. "Here are two *tomans*. Don't lose them. And don't forget to bring back the change."

Abbas put the two *tomans* in his shirt pocket.

"Don't stop to play," his mother called. "Watch out for wild dogs. And hurry. Your father will be soon."

Men squatted on the main street, telling old fables. Abbas listened. He knew all the stories, but every man told them differently. When one began the story of the camel's lunch, Abbas remembered his errand.

Then he heard the sharp, squeaky noise that meant only one thing. The toy man was in town!

The toy man balances a tray of toys on his head. He has bouncing chickens on sticks, pinwheels, whistles, dolls, and other wonderful things made of wood, paper, and clay. He carries a squeeze box that shrills and calls the children to see his toys.

Around the corner, the children following the toy man were ooh-ing and ah-ing. Abbas could see why. On the tray was a most beautiful pinwheel. It was decorated with bits of mirror. As it whirled, it looked like diamonds and shooting stars.

The toy man lifted the heavy tray from his head and sat down under a plane tree. Without the breeze, the pinwheel stopped. Abbas saw the design made by the mirror chips.

"Please, toy man, how much is the beautiful pinwheel?" asked Abbas.

The toy man looked at Abbas's clean but shabby clothes. He leaned back, closing his eyes.

"How much, toy man?" repeated Abbas.

"Two *tomans*," said the toy man without opening his eyes.

Abbas felt the *tomans* in his pocket. Hearing coins jingling, the toy man was suddenly wide-awake. He waved the pinwheel until it spun. In the sunlight it seemed to give off sparks.

"Just two *tomans*," the toy man wheedled. "It's the only one of its kind in the world. No prince has a pinwheel like this one!"

Abbas was silent for a long moment. Then he said, "Excuse me, toy man, I must buy *sangak*. But I'm sure you are right that it's the only one like it in the world." He started away.

"Don't go!" said the toy man. "You look like a nice boy so I'll let you have it for only one *toman*."

Again, Abbas felt in his pocket. "Thank you," he said finally. "But I don't have that much money—of my own. Maybe someday."

Abbas hurried to the bake shop. He ran all the way home, carrying the sheets of *sangak* over his arm.

Abbas's mother was outside the gate. "Where have you been?" she asked. "Your father is waiting! What were you doing?"

Abbas wanted to talk about the beautiful pin-wheel, but he knew that was no excuse. He also knew they had no spare *tomans* for a toy. He hung his head and said nothing.

Abbas's mother gave him part of a *sangak*. "No meat for you today!" she cried. "Here is your lunch. Take it. And don't leave the compound!"

Abbas climbed the plane tree by the gate. He put his *sangak* on the compound wall.

Up in the branches, it was cool and quiet. Most people rested after lunch. There was only the sound of barking dogs. Abbas closed his eyes, remembering the beautiful pinwheel. How it had sparkled! Abbas dreamed he heard the toy man's squeeze box.

Then Abbas realized that he did hear the toy man. He also heard the sound of running feet and the wild dogs barking. What was happening? The toy man didn't come out when people were resting!

Abbas slid quickly from the tree to the wall. He saw the toy man running. Three big dogs were snapping at his legs. He held the tray on his head with one hand. As he ran, he tried to kick back at the snarling dogs.

"Toy man!" Abbas screamed. "Come to the green gate!"

Abbas tore his *sangak* in half. When the toy man was near the gate, Abbas threw one piece across the road. Two of the dogs left the toy man. They growled and fought over the bread. Then Abbas dropped the other piece. The third dog grabbed it and ran.

Abbas jumped down and opened the gate. The

toy man came in. He was breathless. His shoulders sagged as he wearily put the toy tray on the grass.

Abbas brought the toy man a cup of water from the well. The toy man sat down and sipped slowly. Abbas looked closely at the mirrored pinwheel. It was the most beautiful pinwheel in the whole world.

"Thank you for rescuing me," said the toy man.

"It was my pleasure," said Abbas politely.

"Haven't I seen you before?" asked the toy man.

"Yes," said Abbas. "I admired your toys, especially the pinwheel."

"Your family must be rich if you can waste *sangak* on dogs," said the toy man. "Though I'm very glad you did," he added.

"No, we are not rich," said Abbas. "My father is the gardener for the landlord. And the best gardener in the village, too."

Abbas didn't want to talk about giving away his lunch.

"Excuse me," he said. "I have to go now."

"Wait!" said the toy man.

Abbas slipped into the cottage.

When Abbas came out to help his father with the afternoon watering, the toy man was gone.

But in the grass where he had rested, the mirrored pinwheel stood. In the soft breeze, it whirled and looked like diamonds and shooting stars.

A Mysterious Eskimo Name

By Lorna Milne

"Akerta is a strange Eskimo name," Ryann thought as she pulled her parka over her head. "Why did the other sixth graders name me Akerta? It makes me stand out, and I stand out enough as it is."

From her Yup'ik Eskimo teacher, Vivian, Ryann knew that *akerta* meant "sun." But none of the other children had names that meant something besides a name. Her friend Martha's Eskimo name was Nallunaq. A month before Martha was born, an old village woman named Nallunaq had died. The villagers believed that the spirit of the last person to

65

die entered newborn babies, so Martha was named after the woman. Two of the fifth graders were named Nallunaq as well.

Ryann was born in New Hampshire, and had lived there until a year ago. She could not imagine naming a child after someone who had recently died. The thought of it really gave her the willies.

In the coatroom Ryann found her boots, pulled them on, and unfolded the ruff of her hood to protect her face from the wind. She pushed open first one, then the second heavy metal door that led outside to the dark. Loose snow no longer skittered across the ground like sand in the desert. The wind had died since this morning.

Ryann turned back her wolfskin ruff and looked around. She had stayed late, studying in the school's tiny library. The playground was empty. A full amber moon rose in the east over the village of Nunachuk. The porch light was on at her house. She'd tell her mom about the full moon and about her Eskimo name.

As Ryann passed the village store, a boy playing on the steps yelled, "*Cama-i,* Akerta." It took Ryann a moment to recognize her new Eskimo name and respond. She raised a mittened hand in greeting, too shy to call out the boy's Eskimo name, and trudged on down the boardwalk toward home. "Akerta," she mumbled, trying to get used to the sound.

Ryann found her mother behind their two-room

house, hovering over a tripod and camera. Her mother glanced over her shoulder. "Hi," she said. "I've been listening for you. I wanted you to see the moon. Would you like to take a look?"

"Sure," Ryann said. Her mother steadied the tripod in the snow, peeked through the viewer, then stepped out of the way. The moon, now dusty white, filled the frame. Ryann saw the dark blotches of craters, the makings of a face.

"What's the Yup'ik word for moon?" Ryann asked.

Her mother peered through the viewer again, refocused, then pushed the button at the end of the shutter cable. The camera's shutter opened and closed slowly. "*Iraluq.*"

"*Iraluq,*" Ryann repeated. "Did you know *akerta* is the word for sun?"

"Yes, my students taught me *akerta* and *iraluq* when we were translating stories for the school newspaper."

"Mom," Ryann hesitated, "today my class gave me an Eskimo name."

"They did? What is it?"

"Akerta."

"Ryann! That's a wonderful name." Her mother pushed the shutter button again.

"Why would they name me after the sun?"

"Didn't they explain?"

"They spoke in Yup'ik. I can't understand what they're saying when they talk fast."

"You'll understand soon enough. Do you know it's an honor to be given an Eskimo name? I don't have one. Neither does Dad. Bob does, but he has lived here for thirteen years. You're still a *cheechako,* a newcomer."

Bob was the school principal, a tall, gangling man. He was one of eleven white people who lived here in the tundra village among the Eskimos of southwest Alaska. Ryann liked him. He looked as out of place as she did. Bob was a head taller than any of the Eskimos. At least Ryann wasn't very tall.

"What's Bob's Eskimo name?" she asked.

"I don't remember. You can ask him tomorrow." Her mother leaned over and hugged her. "Dry fish for supper? Dipped in seal oil? From now on it's Eskimo food for you, Akerta."

It was still dark when Ryann walked to school the next day. The sun wouldn't rise until 9:45, just as Yup'ik class began. She wondered if she would recognize her name. She'd really have to pay attention. "Akerta," she practiced.

After putting away her parka and boots, Ryann walked down the hall toward the office to find Bob. The hallway and the office were empty, and her footsteps echoed in the semidarkness.

Most of the teachers and students who came early were at breakfast. She decided to go visit her dad in the woodshop, where he was building a dogsled with his students. He had left home to work on it even before Ryann was out of bed.

In the shop Bob was helping Ryann's dad bend the sled handle around the specially built frame. When they finished, they turned to greet her.

"Good morning, Akerta," her dad said cheerfully. Ryann frowned.

"Bob, what's your Eskimo name?" she blurted out.

"Yugpak. Why?" Bob asked.

"Yugpak? Does that mean something?"

"It means 'giant,'" Bob said, smiling.

"Why did they give you a name that means giant?" Ryann asked.

"Because to the villagers, I'm very tall. Like a giant," Bob said.

Ryann studied Bob for a minute. "I have to go," she said, and hurried out the door. "I'm glad my class didn't give me a name like giant," Ryann thought. She headed for her room.

Sitting at her desk, Ryann watched as Vivian pinned the Solar System on a bulletin board for the morning science lesson. Only the moon, earth, and sun had Eskimo as well as English names.

Her classmates began to fill the desks in front of her, their black heads glistening like ripe crowberries in the rain. Thoughtfully, Ryann reached up and felt the thick, bright yellow braid that her mother had plaited down her back.

"Akerta," she said softly.

Cowbells
and
Paintbrushes

By Loretta Romanek

It was the end of May in the Swiss town of Alpen-stein. The farmers were about to begin their journey to the high mountain meadows above the tree line. Each year they herded their cows to these fresh summer pastures. Men and boys lived in mountain barns and huts until the first snows of another winter forced them to return to the valleys below.

Peter Clause paused in the kitchen doorway. His father was busily packing the flour, sugar, and salt they would need at the summer farm.

"Papa?"

"What is it, Peter?"

"In which bundle should I put my paints?"

Peter's father stopped working and turned to his son. "We are farmers—not artists," he said shortly.

"But I love both," said Peter, "painting and farming."

His father shook his head. "You may use that sack over there by the stove. I don't see how you will have time for painting anyway. Now prepare for tomorrow, for I have work to do."

There were many things Peter wanted to paint— the green meadows covered with blue and yellow wild flowers, the snowy peaks, the little cheese-making hut. He gazed up at the mountains, half-hidden in mist, towering above the tiny village. "I'll find a way," he said to himself. "I'm strong. I can do my work and my painting. There has to be time for both."

The long, hard climb began early the next morning. The tinkling of cowbells and the shouts of men and boys filled the air. The procession followed the path that led from the village, upward through pine forests to the high mountain passes.

As they neared the farm, Peter's excitement grew. "There it is!" he cried as he raced past the cows and goats that had made the long trip with them. "Everything is perfect! Papa, look at the mountain peaks with the last bit of sunlight shining on them. Isn't it beautiful up here?"

His father nodded thoughtfully. "Yes, it is good to be back. But now we must settle the animals for the night. There is much to do."

Peter worked hard at the summer farm, from before the sun rose until long after it had disappeared behind the distant peaks. Yet every night, while his father lay sleeping in the hayloft above, Peter carefully brought out his tubes of paint and his brushes. By the dim light of a candle, he would paint until he could no longer remain awake.

As the days passed, he grew weary from lack of sleep. One morning his father had difficulty arousing him. "Peter, wake up! It is already five o'clock!"

"I'm coming," mumbled Peter sleepily. He brushed the loose hay from his hair and clothing and struggled down the hayloft ladder.

After lighting a fire, he poured coffee and milk into a large pot. As it was heating, he unwrapped cheese and bread and laid them on the table.

During breakfast, Peter's father watched him intently. "Perhaps you should return to the valley," he said in a low voice.

Startled by his father's words, Peter cried out, "Please, let me stay. I love being here."

"But you do not look well, Peter. You are tired, and your face is without color."

"But I'm working hard," said Peter. "I finish all my chores."

"It is not the work I am concerned with; it's you."

"Let me stay just a little longer," begged Peter.

His father continued eating his bread and cheese. He raised his bowl of hot coffee and milk to his lips and emptied it. Then he stood up and buttoned his heavy wool shirt. "All right, a little longer." He strode out of the hut.

Peter stared at the empty doorway. "Papa is right," he thought sadly. "I can't do both. When I return to the valley, I will begin painting again. For now, I will be a farmer only."

He wrapped the cheese in a cloth and washed the bowls.

A week later, after having milked the cows, Peter trudged to the cheese-making hut. A light snow was falling, disappearing as it touched the ground.

He stamped his muddy boots on a board near the door and went inside. There he saw his father gazing at his paintings, which lay upon the table.

"You painted these, Peter?"

"Yes, Papa."

Peter's father studied the paintings. "I have been a foolish man," he said, slowly shaking his head.

Peter watched him, puzzled.

"You have spoken for me, Peter. Here, in your paintings, is my love for the mountains." His father ran his fingers lightly over the canvas. "When did you find time to paint these?" he asked.

"I used to paint at night, but I no longer do that," answered Peter.

"I see," said his father. "That is why you were so tired. Nighttime is for sleeping, especially after working as hard as you do. From now on, you will paint during the day."

Peter couldn't believe it. He wanted to run to his father and hug him. Instead, he smiled gratefully, and his father understood.

"I would like to continue looking at these pictures of yours. Do you think we could hang them on the wall?" asked his father.

They hammered nails into the rough beams and hung the paintings. "What a cheese-making hut we have," said Peter, laughing.

His father put his arm around Peter's shoulder. "Who says a farmer can't be an artist!"

Drumbeats
for Danger

By Marlene Richardson

The sun beat down on the plain. The heat rose up in shimmering waves. Hardly a creature stirred, for it was the hottest part of the day. Sleepily, the lion opened one eye at the sound of the growl from his mate. The cubs were making a game of catching their mother's tail as she brushed the flies off herself. Unconcerned by her first warning, the cubs were now crouched, waiting to spring again. Swish, swish went her tail; temptation was too great! With delight they pounced once more, biting her tail with their sharp teeth. Very annoyed, his mate snarled at the cubs, and cuffing them with her paws, she sent them scurrying off to the shade of another tree.

The disturbance over, the lion closed his eyes, settling back for his afternoon nap. Happily, he drifted off to sleep, only to be awakened by the sound of drums beating in the distance. The sound of man! He felt that familiar sensation of fear, but at the same time the drumbeats seemed to stir up vague memories from his past—memories he couldn't quite recapture. The drumbeats were too far away to be any immediate danger, but he could not relax. The safety of his family was at stake.

How could that lion know that those beating drums were indeed a terrible threat? They were calling out the news that Bwanga, son of the chief, would soon go through the ritual of manhood. It was the custom of this tribe that before a youth could be accepted as an adult and warrior, he would have to kill a lion. The courage of the lion was held above all else; to fight one was indeed a badge of courage.

Bwanga and the warriors fanned out across the plains in the formation of a large circle. They had heard the roaring of the lion. Chanting and making loud noises, the circle of men closed in. It would be into this circle that Bwanga would step to prove his courage.

Pacing back and forth nervously, the lion listened

intently to sounds growing closer. His mate was on her feet, with the cubs close at her heels. They, too, could feel the danger in the air. The chanting was coming from all around; the lion was frightened and confused. Which way did safety lie? A decision must be made. He growled at his mate, and they all headed west across the plains. Too late! They were cut off from all escape. The lion's instinct told him that to insure the safety of his family, he must divert attention to himself. Roaring loudly, he ran directly toward the circle of men. Quickly, they closed their ranks. His family was saved, but he was trapped. The lion's heart thumped with fear as he vainly charged the advancing warriors, only to be driven back by their loud chanting.

Suddenly one figure stepped out of the circle advancing toward him. Warily the lion and Bwanga looked at each other. The lion snarled ferociously, but Bwanga moved closer, shield up, jabbing with his spear. Muscles tensed, the lion sprang, missing Bwanga's up-thrust spear by inches! The tribesmen gasped in horror. Bwanga was at the mercy of the enraged lion, and custom would allow no one to help him. This was Bwanga's battle alone.

The warriors' gasps of horror soon turned to ex-clamations of astonishment. They could hardly be-lieve their eyes. Instead of going in for the kill, the lion was now quietly watching Bwanga. The lion's memory, triggered by the smell of Bwanga, had come rushing back. In his past he remembered gentle hands soothing a wound. The lion was confused. How could he kill what he had loved?

Bwanga lay there, panting and stunned. Why had this lion given him a second chance? His eyes scanned the hulk of the lion, and suddenly he spotted the line of the long scar running down the lion's leg. It was Simba—the cub that had not yet been weaned when Bwanga and his father had found him starving and wounded by the body of his dead mother. His mother had been in battle with some horned animal and had died of the wounds. Bwanga and his father had taken Simba to their village and had cared for him until he was old enough to look after himself. Then, sadly, they sent him back to the plains to follow his natural life. It was years ago, but now it seemed like yesterday.

"It is Simba! It is Simba whom we loved!" said Bwanga.

The circle of warriors had grown silent as they watched the lion and Bwanga. It was unbelievable!

As if of one mind, the men opened a path for this beautiful lion. With relief, Simba made a dash for freedom back to the life he loved, the open plains and his family.

Bwanga looked fondly at the retreating lion, the lion that had given him back his life. Bwanga's test of courage was over, and it had taught him a lesson he would never forget. What a foolish price to pay for courage! There was no sense to this test of kill or be killed. Old ways were hard to change, but when he became chief, man and animal would live together in freedom.

Juan's Gift

By Bernadine Beatie

The large baskets hanging from each side of a yoke across Juan's shoulders were only half-full when he stopped by the shop of Señor Martinez.

"*¡Halo!*" Juan called, hoping that Señor Martinez would answer instead of his son, Carlos. Carlos was only a few years older than Juan, but he was always trying to get Juan to cut his price for delivering merchandise to the market in the city. Indeed, everyone in the village said that Carlos watched his pesos so carefully that he would one day be the richest man in all of Mexico. Carlos often called Juan a spend-thrift. Juan supposed he was. Pesos certainly had a way of slipping through his fingers.

"*Buenos días,* Juan," Señor Martinez called. He and Carlos came from the shop, carrying two boxes filled with pottery shaped like pigs and painted with bright flowers.

"I wish you could carry more," Señor Martinez said. "We have several orders that must be filled by tomorrow."

Juan grinned. "Tomorrow, señor, I can carry them all. Today I am buying a burro!"

Carlos shrugged. "I have heard that before. The last time you had money enough for a burro you brought home paints and canvas for your friend Pepe. And the time before, two small lambs for the old Señora Juanita."

"Juan's money was well spent," Señor Martinez said. "Pepe has been a different lad since then. Some-day he will be a fine artist. And Señora Juanita is always the first to come when anyone in the village needs help."

"But if Juan spends his money foolishly instead of buying a burro," said Carlos, "we will have to hire someone else to make our deliveries."

"I suppose so," Señor Martinez said sadly.

"Do not worry, señor," Juan cried. "I have already selected a burro. His name is Benito. He is at Señor

Perez's auction barn."

"I will believe that when I see the burro," Carlos said.

"You will see!" Juan cried. "I will buy this burro, then another, and another. Someday I will deliver glass and pottery for every shop in the village."

Carlos shook his head. "No, Juan. You will always be a poor one like the old señora. She is good and kind, *sí*; but she has nothing to show for it but a poor house, the lambs you gave her, and a small black-and-white dog, too old to be of any use."

Juan walked down the village street. He would show Carlos. He would not be poor all of his life. From now on he would guard each peso. He started whistling a happy tune.

Ahead, Juan saw the small adobe house of the old señora. He expected to see her sweeping the yard or watering the bright flowers blooming in cracked pots and pans, with her dog, Paco, at her heels. Instead she stood at the gate alone, tears rolling down her cheeks.

"*¡Ay de mí!*" Juan cried, running forward. "Is something wrong with Paco, señora?"

"*Sí*, he did not awaken this morning. But do not worry, Juan. Paco was old and tired. He can rest now," the old señora said. She gave Juan a trembly smile and turned away.

Juan's heart was heavy as he walked on. How lonely the old señora would be without Paco. He was still thinking of her when he stopped at the auction barn at the edge of the city.

"¡Halo!" Señor Perez called out. "Did you come for your burro, Juan?"

"Sí, señor," Juan said and counted out the pesos into Señor Perez's hand.

"Benito is tied inside the barn," Señor Perez said.

"I'll fetch him," Juan said.

When Juan stepped inside the barn, he heard a low, eager whining coming from a cage near the door. He smiled. A small black-and-white dog, tail wagging furiously, was thrusting a nose through the slats. The dog looked so much like the old señora's Paco that Juan gave a whistle of surprise.

"Do you want a sheep dog, Juan?" Señor Perez spoke from the door.

"How much does he cost?" Juan asked.

"The same as your burro."

Juan's eyes widened. "So many pesos for a small dog?"

Señor Perez shrugged. "A sheep dog is cheap at that price, Juan."

An hour later Juan reached the market. He was not leading a burro. Instead, the small black-and-white dog was sleeping on top of one of the loaded baskets. Juan smiled each time he thought of how happy the old señora would be, and how surprised. "I am lucky, too," Juan thought. For when Señor Perez learned that he was buying the dog for the old señora, he had promised to keep Benito until Juan had saved more pesos.

"I know the old señora," Señor Perez had said. "Once long ago, when my small Anita was sick, Señora Juanita came all this way with herbs to stop the fever. She is a great lady, that one!"

Only when he neared home late that afternoon did Juan start worrying. If Señor Martinez hired someone else to make his deliveries, it would be a very long time before he could save enough money to buy his burro.

As Juan neared the village, he heard laughter and the sound of music. He paused in surprise to see the old señora's yard filled with visitors. Everyone in the village was there, even Señor Martinez and Carlos. The old señora sat on the porch like a queen, with Pepe beside her. Juan's heart bounded. The old señora's friends had heard of her sadness and had come to comfort her.

Carlos spied Juan and hurried toward him. "I see a dog," he said, "but not a burro."

Juan lifted the dog into his arms. "He is like Paco," he said. "Will not the old señora be happy?" And he ran forward to place the small dog in the old señora's arms.

"*¡Ah, ay!*" she cried happily. "It is almost as if I were holding the small Paco."

Carlos came to stand beside Juan. "You will always be poor, Juan. You will never have a burro."

The old señora overheard. "Now is the time, Pepe!" she cried.

Pepe rose and walked around the house. He was back in a moment, leading a small burro with a garland of flowers about its neck.

"Benito!" Juan cried. "It is Benito!"

"*Sí,* Juan," the old señora said, smiling. "Señor Perez was so pleased that you put my happiness before your own that he brought Benito here early this afternoon."

"But I cannot pay for him—not yet," Juan cried.

"Your friends will help," Pepe said, smiling. "I sold two of my pictures."

"And I sold a serape woven from the wool of the two small lambs," the old señora said.

"Juan shall have my business as long as he wants it!" Señor Martinez cried out, shaking a finger under Carlos's nose.

There was a strange look on Carlos's face—a lost, lonely look. The old señora reached out and placed a gentle hand on his shoulder. "No one is poor, Carlos, when he has friends," she said softly.

The Ups and Downs of Being Luis

By Karen Mollett

It's not easy being me. When I was nine life was simple. But now my shirts don't fit because my arms are too long. My pants don't fit because my legs are too long. My hair is so short that my hat doesn't even fit. I don't fit into my clothes anymore, and I don't fit into my family.

I live with my mom, an older sister, and a younger brother. I'm the middle kid, and there's just not enough room for a middle kid. We live with my

Aunt Rosa and two cousins. My cousin Ernesto is even older than my sister. My other cousin is a girl and just a baby. My grandma is with us, which means eight of us live in an apartment in what my teacher calls an "urban area."

I love my family, but I need some space. When I want to be alone, I walk through the alleys of my neighborhood.

And that's how I found the umbrella. It was so huge that when I finally got it open, I could hide behind it. It was bright orange with blue, red, green, and yellow parrots painted on it. Standing behind it with the sun coming through was like standing behind the stained-glass window at church.

I decided to take the umbrella home, open it in the apartment, and make a space where I could go to be by myself. No kid should have to hang out in an alley just to get some peace.

I slipped into the apartment and stood by the door. The babies were playing on the rug in front of the sofa. Grandma was reading the paper at the table in the nook. I could hear my mom and Aunt Rosa fixing dinner. I figured Angie, my sister, was in the girls' room, studying.

"Ernesto, turn that radio down! I can't hear myself think!" she screeched, pounding on the wall.

Ernesto turned down the volume of the radio just long enough to make a loud, rude noise that sent Angie wailing to Mom.

This was home all right. I opened the umbrella and sat down behind it. With my back to the wall and my umbrella in front of me, I waited.

The baby noticed first, and she started crying.

"Birdy! Birdy!" my brother shouted, jumping up and down.

I dived around the umbrella and grabbed him. "Don't touch it!" I shouted.

Grandma dropped the paper to the table with a thud. "Luis, where on earth—?"

Ernesto interrupted her when he came from the boys' room.

Feeling mean, I put down the baby and got ready to fight them all for my umbrella.

Ernesto looked at me, then at the umbrella, then back at me. "Luis, it's great," he said, getting behind it and pulling me back there with him.

Angie poked her head around the side of the umbrella. "Luis, it is totally awesome," she said.

"Totally awful," Aunt Rosa muttered as she took the crying baby to the back of the apartment.

Grandma was holding my brother and running her hand over one of the parrots. "Well, I'll be. They're painted on," she said.

Ernesto punched my arm. "I have shop tomorrow. I'll get a couple of hooks, and we can hang it from the ceiling right in front of the window," he said, looking excited.

"I want to use it like a tent," I grumbled. "I want it

for my private space," I added, not wanting them to like my umbrella.

"Hey, well . . ." He thought a minute. "We could rig up a pulley. Then you can lower the umbrella when you need the privacy or leave it up for the sun to shine through. Well, Luis, what do you say?"

Everyone looked hopeful. I said yes, and that night Mom helped me sew two long pieces of cord to my umbrella.

The next afternoon Ernesto had two eye screws. He climbed a ladder and put both of them into the ceiling. We ran the cords from the umbrella through the eye screws in the ceiling.

At the count of three Ernesto and I pulled the cords, raising the umbrella until it touched the ceiling. Ernesto came around the table and tied my side for me. Then we joined everyone else.

The sun was shining through all of those colors, and I had to admit it was beautiful. "It's just like having a stained-glass window," Mom said softly.

I felt sort of strange. A thing I had hoped would keep me away from my family had somehow made me a part of my family.

That was a month ago. I haven't wanted the umbrella down yet, but I probably will tonight. I've got my report card right here, and I think I need some privacy.

Dishpan Ducks

By Margaret Springer

Rosa walked home from school slowly. She did not have one friend. She did not like this new country. The people talked too fast in their language. The rows of apartment buildings and the streets full of cars looked all the same. And it was cold.

Rosa missed her country. She missed her friends and her cousins and her grandmothers and her aunts. She missed the trees and the hills and the grass and the flowers. Most of all she missed the animals—the chickens and the goats and the dogs.

Every day Rosa walked to school alone and walked home alone. Gradually, she learned some English, but she did not know what to say or what to do when other kids were around. They were friendly, but Rosa felt safer being alone.

Behind Rosa's brick apartment building was a special place, a small creek where Rosa always stopped after school. Ducks swam there, and Rosa could speak to them in her language. The ducks seemed to understand.

Every afternoon Rosa sat on a concrete slab above the creek and watched the ducks until Mama came home from work.

Rosa did not feed them. She knew that most people food was not right for ducks. But she watched them swim and feed and walk up to her, quacking. Once they even walked over Rosa's tummy as she lay with her feet stretched out on the bumpy grass.

One day after school, the ducks were not in the water. They did not waddle toward Rosa, even though she stayed very still. Something was wrong.

Gently, Rosa tiptoed to where the ducks were huddled. "Are you sick?" she whispered. They looked different. They looked greasy.

Then Rosa noticed the creek. An oily film covered it, making patches of color on the water's surface. She looked closely at the ducks. Their feathers were stuck together. They could not swim.

"I must get help," said Rosa to herself. "But how? I

don't know anyone. Mama told me not to speak to strangers. Besides, I don't know how to ask in English."

Rosa had an idea. She rushed back to the street, walked to the traffic light, then raced around the corner and back to the school yard. Boys and girls were still there, practicing baseball with the gym teacher.

"Please! Come!" said Rosa, breathless. "Ducks!"

"Hello, Rosa," said the teacher. "What's the trouble?"

"Ducks!" said Rosa again. It was one of the few English words she was sure of. "Come. Please. Ducks!"

She pointed in the direction of the creek. The kids were staring at her, but she didn't care. "Ducks!" she said again, her dark eyes pleading.

The teacher said something in English to his team. They looked at Rosa and talked all at once. Then the teacher smiled. "OK, Rosa," he said. "Show us." They all grabbed their baseball mitts and bats and followed Rosa to the creek.

Pretty soon more people were at Rosa's creek than she had ever seen there before. First the police came with their squad cars and sirens. Then came the fire fighters with their big trucks, and the Humane Society workers in their vans.

People came out from the apartment building with dishpans and towels and liquid dish detergent. Rosa did not understand all the talk, but she knew what was happening.

The ducks were too weak to fly or run away. Rosa and the other kids rounded them up and held them in the dishpans while Humane Society people worked. Each duck was washed four times with mild detergent, and rinsed four times with water.

After a while someone brought a blow-dryer. Rosa laughed as the ducks were blown fluffy-dry. One by one, they were placed carefully into cages in the Humane Society vans.

"We'll keep them for a few days," one of the workers said. "They need time to regain the natural oils in their feathers, so they can keep themselves warm and swim properly. A big factory upstream spilled four hundred gallons of diesel fuel into the storm sewers last night. What a mess! You got to these ducks just in time, young lady."

Rosa did not know what the man was saying, but she saw everyone smile at her, and she felt proud.

By the time Rosa's mama came home, the cars and the vans and the people were gone. Rosa was in her special place by the creek. But she was not alone. She was playing baseball with three friends. Rosa was good at baseball. She was getting better at English, too.

"Home run!" she shouted, laughing, after she slugged the ball almost to the parking lot.

Rosa was happy. And the dishpan ducks were safe.